KB150233

CLASSICO

Part of Cow & Bridge Publishing Co.
Web site : www.cafe.naver.com/sowadari
3ga-302, 6-21, 40th St., Guwolro, Namgu, Incheon, #402-848 South Korea
Telephone 0505-719-7787 Facsimile 0505-719-7788 Email sowadari@naver.com

The Story of
A FIERCE BAD RABBIT
by Beatrix Potter

Published by Cow & Bridge Publishing Co.
First original edition published by Frederick Warne & Co. London
This recovery edition published by Cow & Bridge Publishing Co. Korea

ISBN 978-89-98046-49-1

사납고 못된 토끼 이야기

베아트릭스 포터 지음

Cow & Bridge
PUBLISHING COMPANY

오늘은
사납고 못된 토끼 이야기를
해 줄게요.

요 사납고 못된 토끼 좀 보세요.
빳빳한 수염, 뾰쪽한 발톱
치켜세운 꼬리!

얌전하고 착한 토끼.

엄마가 주신

맛있는 당근.

사납고 못된 토끼는
너무너무 당근이
먹고 싶었어요.

"이리 내!"
사납고 못된 토끼가
당근을 빼앗아요.
"나도 좀 줄래?"
라고 해야지!

사납고 못된 토끼가
얌전하고 착한 토끼를
세게 밀쳐 버려요.

불쌍한 착한 토끼는
무서워서 굴 속으로
숨어 버려요.

기다란 총을 든
무서운 사냥꾼 아저씨.

"의자 위에 저게 뭐지?
이상하게도 생겼구나."

23

사냥꾼 아저씨가
나무 뒤에 숨었다가
살금살금 다가와서

기다란 총으로

"빵!"

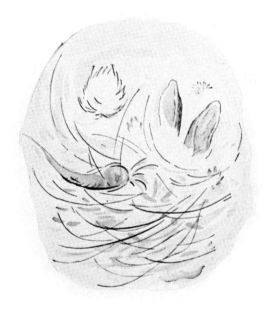

아이코, 깜짝이야.

이게 무슨 일이지요?

헐레벌떡 뛰어오는
사냥꾼 아저씨.
의자 위에 남은 건
당근하고 수염하고
복실한 꼬리.

얌전하고 착한 토끼는

굴 속에 숨어 있었고요.

꼬리가 떨어진
사납고 못된 토끼는
우앙우앙 울면서
도망쳤대요.

따라 해 보세요.

"나도 좀 줄래?"

"그래, 같이 먹자."

–끝–

베아트릭스 포터
스케치 앨범

My rabbit Peter is so lazy, he lies before
the fire in a box, with a little rug.
His claws grew too long,
quite uncomfortable,
so I tried to cut them with scissors
. but they were so hard that I
had to use the big gardens scissors
He sat quite still and
allowed me to do his
little front paws but
when I cut the other hind foot claws

, +

aughty.

wild rabbit digging holes

worn

not wild

rabbits throwing snow balls.

but so proud!
I meet him
out shopping in the morning, he looks at
me sideways but he never speaks

sleep right at the top of a haw-
thorn bush, the
branches are quite
covered with chickens. Those at
the farm go up a
stone wall into a
loft. The farmer

has a beautiful fat pig. He is a
funny old man,
he feeds the calves
every morning, he
rattles the spoon on the tin pail, to
tell them breakfast is ready, but
they won't always come, then there is a
noise like a German band. I remain
yrs. aff. Beatrix Potter.

MR 2001 (51)

Miss Hayward
keeps the
house but
it really does belong to Stumpy
it is quite a pretty story.
Once upon
a time

there was an old clergyman, who
had no family, and Stumpy was

The sparrows are naughty,
they pull off the
flowers. There are

two nests, just under the
gutter at the top
of our house. We
see them flying up
with grass to make the
nest. We do not like it because
the little birds fall out
onto our door-steps.

I hope that you and Eric
will have a very good time, and with
love I remain yrs. aff. Beatrix Potter

MA 2009 (7)

오리지널 피터래빗 시리즈 10
The Story of a Fierce Bad Rabbit
사납고 못된 토끼 이야기

1판 1쇄 2014년 12월 5일
지은이 베아트릭스 포터 **옮긴이** 김동근
발행인 김동근
발행처 소와다리
출판등록 제2011-000015호(2011년 8월 3일)
주소 인천광역시 남구 구월로 40번길 6-21번지 3가동 302호
전화 0505-719-7787
팩스 0505-719-7788
이메일 sowadari@naver.com

파본은 구입처를 통해 바꿔드립니다.

ISBN 978-89-98046-49-1